A BOY NAMED QUEEN

A BOY NAMED
QUEEN

SARA CASSIDY

Groundwood Books
House of Anansi Press
Toronto Berkeley

Published in Canada and the USA in 2016 by Groundwood Books
First paperback edition 2019

Thank you to Groundwood editor Shelley Tanaka for her thorough,
thoughtful attention. — SC

Groundwood Books / House of Anansi Press
groundwoodbooks.com

We gratefully acknowledge for their financial support of our publishing program
the Canada Council for the Arts, the Ontario Arts Council and the Government
of Canada.

Canada Council
for the Arts
Conseil des Arts
du Canada

ONTARIO ARTS COUNCIL
CONSEIL DES ARTS DE L'ONTARIO
an Ontario government agency
un organisme du gouvernement de l'Ontario

With the participation of the Government of Canada
Avec la participation du gouvernement du Canada | Canadä

Library and Archives Canada Cataloguing in Publication

Title: A boy named Queen / Sara Cassidy.
Names: Cassidy, Sara, author.
Description: First paperback edition.
Identifiers: Canadiana 2019015554X | ISBN 9781773063782 (softcover)
Classification: LCC PS8555 A7812 B69 2020 | DDC jC813/.54—dc23

Cover design by Michael Solomon
Cover art © Betsy Everitt, i2iart.com

Groundwood Books is committed to protecting our natural environment. As
part of our efforts, the interior of this book is printed on paper that contains
100% post-consumer recycled fibers, is acid-free and is processed chlorine-free.

Printed and bound in Canada

For Chloe, Finnerty and Sophia

1

Evelyn has forgotten how to fold up the lawn chair. Push? Pull?

Right. One hand on the back, press a knee here, yank upward and ...

Ouch! Evelyn shakes her hand hard as if she can fling out the pain. She puts her throbbing finger in her mouth and sucks, gazing up.

It is a bright Tuesday. The sky is perfectly clear. No popcorn bursts, no cottony fistfuls of chair stuffing, not a single down feather. Only strange patches where the blue is so light that when Evelyn peers into them they lose color completely. They're like windows or tunnels. Maybe to outer space!

Click-click. A sparrow scrabbles for a hold on the birdfeeder's short peg. Two more chairs to fold.

As always on the last day of summer holidays, Evelyn and her parents have spent the morning scrubbing their brown two-bedroom house that stands in a row of other brown two-bedroom houses. They've coiled the hose. They've packaged up the badminton net with its rackets and birdies (Evelyn's mother, who is Scottish, calls them shuttlecocks) and stowed everything tidily in the garage.

Finally, Evelyn's mother pronounces the house neat as a new pin.

Lunch is tomato soup. Evelyn's father breaks his crackers into his bowl so the pieces float like icebergs on a red sea. Evelyn thinks it's rude of her father to dump his crackers in his soup, as if he's lazy and in a hurry at the same time. It's like when he cleans the wax from his ears with the end of his eyeglasses.

10

Evelyn's mother never breaks her crackers. She's never in a hurry. She is *on top of things*. One of her habits is to press the last scrap of the old bar of soap onto the new bar. Although the soap in Evelyn's house is humpbacked, no soap is ever wasted.

"Let's get our ducks in a row," Evelyn's mother says now.

She places three teacups on the table. Evelyn's father pours tea from his cup into his saucer, then blows, rippling the surface of the shallow brown pond. He lifts the pond to his lips and slurps.

"After lunch, your father will wash the car. Evelyn and I will go to Frederick's for shoes."

Evelyn's mother once read that children's feet grow fastest in summer, so Evelyn spends July and August in open-toed sandals. She loved this year's pair: straps of white leather that softened as her skin browned. But now her toes hang over the ends a little.

Evelyn and her mother walk to Frederick's once a year. It's as sure as Christmas. The day hovers between summer and fall, the warm air stirred every so often by a cool breeze.

Suddenly, Evelyn's mother sinks into a bench.

"Och, no," she moans. She touches her heart and nods across the street. "Evie, look."

Evelyn blinks. Frederick's Footwear is no more. The store has been blasted with fluorescent light. The wooden sign with swoopy letters is gone. Instead, a plastic sign with plain letters says BUDGET SHOES.

"What can we do," Evelyn's mother says, standing up. Evelyn wedges her hand under her mother's elbow. The two step bravely into the street.

The brass bell on the top of the door has been removed. Instead, Evelyn and her mother are beeped in. Evelyn studies the plastic speaker low on the doorframe. Infrared. An invisible tripwire.

She'd like to try entering the store without triggering it. Bellycrawl like a marine. Or maybe a kung fu scissors jump would do the trick.

The biggest surprise is Mr. Schumann. He's still here with his watery eyes and grayish skin

12

and hair in his ears like packed snow. But he isn't dressed in his usual brown three-piece suit. Instead he wears a T-shirt! With a nametag: *Right Fit Technician. FRED.*

"Perhaps it's better this way," Evelyn's mother tells Mr. Schumann soothingly, after he explains the changes, mentioning "buy out" and "franchise" — a word that to Evelyn sounds like something pretending to be sweet.

After searching the half-empty shelves, Evelyn's mother finally reaches for a pair of blue canvas shoes.

Evelyn freezes. If she moves, a truck will pull up with a delivery of stiff leather loafers, the kind that have dug at her ankles every year since kindergarten.

The blue shoes in her mother's hands are neither leather nor loafer. They're like runners. Lace-ups, of course. Evelyn's mother would never buy shoes with Velcro.

Velcro, she says, is for a different kind of family.

"Let's get you into the Brannock device," Mr. Schumann says, kneeling.

Evelyn removes her beloved sandals. After the long hot summer, the leather insoles bear the imprint of her toes, permanent oval shadows. Evelyn's mother hands her a horrible clot of stocking that reaches halfway up her shin, and Evelyn places her right heel in the cool metal bowl marked R.

Mr. Schumann adjusts the levers, squeezing her foot snugly just for a moment. He swings the device around and lowers Evelyn's left heel into the bowl marked L.

"Still just the two feet?" he asks.

Evelyn smiles. Even with the T-shirt, it's still jokey Mr. Schumann.

"Looks like you've been eating your schnitzel. You've become a size five."

"And I'm going into grade five."

"The stars align."

Mr. Schumann takes the blue shoe and disappears through the curtain into the back. When he emerges, box in hand, his glasses are askew and he's out of breath.

"Here we are," he puffs, reaching into the ruffle

of tissue. "The last pair. It's a half-size down, but the sizing is wild with these offshore shoes. We may be all right."

Evelyn slips her feet into the near-runners. When her mother prods the ends, she draws back her toes.

"Take them for a test drive," Mr. Schumann says.

"Yes, Evie, take a spin. Give them a whirl."

Evelyn's mother and Mr. Schumann get along in a way that her mother and father don't. Evelyn thinks it's because they're both from Europe. The Old World. Evelyn's father is from Alberta.

The near-runners feel entirely different from loafers. They bend with her feet. The soles are like licorice instead of breadboards.

Ha! Breadboards! LOAFers! Evelyn stifles a smile.

"They're good," she says as calmly as she can, as her heart thrums.

"You can wear them home," her mother says. She reaches into her purse. "Does this modern establishment respect hard cash? Or only plastic?"

"Anything that's money," Mr. Schumann says.

Evelyn lets out her breath. Her feet have graduated! She'll be able to play field hockey in these shoes.

She hands her old sandals to Mr. Schumann, who tells her they'll go into the store's new high-efficiency incinerator.

Every step home, Evelyn's toes bang into the ends of her new shoes. But she says nothing. After all, as her mother would say, it's *her own doing*. Besides, her sandals are going up in flames. She can never have them back.

Her outfit for the first day of school is neatly folded at the end of her bed. If she stretches she can wedge her toes under the quiet pile. A new green T-shirt, new jean skirt and new blue tights. The blue shoes are side by side on the floor.

As she drifts off to sleep, a smoky picture comes to mind.

A pile of ash studded with two blackened buckles.

2

Evelyn fiddles with the stiff plastic clasp on her pencil case, snapping it open, buckling it shut. She likes to press her fingertips against the pointy nibs of this year's army of colored pencils, then watch as the indents refill, as if her fingers are inflating. By the end of the year, she knows the pencils will lie broken on the battlefield that is the bottom of her backpack, and the grade five class of Hillsberry Elementary will be noisy and messy with misplaced snacks and dying bean plants and models made with toilet-paper tubes.

For now, though, the room is bright and echoey. Everyone sits up straight in their seats. Socks are pulled high. Braids are tight. Eyeglasses are squeaky clean.

Tap-shh-tap. The teacher writes his name on the board: Mr. Zhang.

Snap! The year's first chalk stick snaps in two. Isabella Perez dives under Khalid Ahmar's desk to retrieve the fallen half, dirtying the knees of her new pink jeans.

To keep her mind off her toes aching in her tight new shoes, Evelyn studies the posters on the classroom walls. In one, a puppy charges down a country road, its ears high with excitement. Fancy letters spell out *Today is the first day of the rest of your life.*

That's perfectly true, Evelyn thinks. And yesterday was the last day of my old life.

Chalk dust blooms from Mr. Zhang's hands as he claps for the students' attention. The dust settles onto the shoulders of his black shirt, making it look as if he has been seasoned by a giant saltshaker. The minute hand on the classroom clock spasms into place, pointing straight up.

Nine o'clock on the nose.

"Welcome to grade five," Mr. Zhang says, pressing his lips into a smile. "I am sure we will have a productive year together."

On the board, he writes out the daily schedule. Evelyn knows that grade five is the end of afternoon recess, but it's still a shock to see it missing from the day's activities.

She looks around the classroom. Nadine Pratt has grown her hair long, which means that Evelyn is the only girl in grade five with short hair. She hopes her mother doesn't find out. What if she makes her grow her hair long, too?

"Now," Mr. Zhang says, reaching for a stack of papers. "Let's see how much math you've forgotten over the holidays."

As Mr. Zhang distributes the quiz, the grade fives reach for their pencils. A few line up at the pencil sharpener. A few more raise their hands and ask to go to the bathroom.

Rap-rap. A knock at the door.

Mrs. Alison, the school secretary, steps into the room.

"Another one," she tells Mr. Zhang. "New to town."

Evelyn and the other students stare as a child with long wavy hair and wearing several bead necklaces steps out from behind Mrs. Alison.

Mrs. Alison raises her eyebrows at Mr. Zhang. "A *boy*."

The boy wears a faded pink T-shirt and jeans with stringy holes in the knees. Poking out from under the ragged cuffs, like a clever joke, is a pair of beautifully polished, pointy-toed black shoes — the kind Evelyn's mother calls brogues. His freckles outnumber even Evelyn's. But they're strong spices — cinnamon, paprika — compared to Evelyn's weak tea stains.

"Welcome," says a flustered Mr. Zhang, glancing at the clock. A sprig of his slick black hair springs out of place and a quiz drifts from his hand to the floor. Isabella once again dirties her pink knees.

"Hello," the boy says, taking in the room of unfamiliar faces. He speaks as though he's on stage, at a microphone, as if he has been invited to give a speech. He isn't nervous at all.

"Tell us," Mr. Zhang asks. "What is your name?"

"My name is Queen," the boy answers.

The grade fives titter.

"Queen?" Mr. Zhang asks. "Q-u-e-e-n. Really?"

"Yes," the boy answers.

Mr. Zhang touches his mouth as if he could push his words back in. "Sorry."

Kids whisper between desks. Queen studies them with steady green eyes as if he knows just what they're saying.

"What brought you to Hillsberry, uh, Queen?" Mr. Zhang asks, barely pronouncing the *n*, turning the boy's name into "Quee."

"Mom and Dad wanted to get away from it all."

"Away from *what* all?" Khalid blurts.

"The rat race," Mr. Zhang says.

"Actually, the rigors of the road," Queen says.

21

"I see." Mr. Zhang clears a pile of books from a desk beside Evelyn. He sweeps his arm across the desktop to dust it off. For the rest of the day, his dark sleeve will be speckled with pink eraser peelings. "Have a seat. At lunch, we'll find you a cubby."

Queen places his backpack beside the desk and sits. Behind him, Connor Linman pokes Parker Simpson and points at Queen's bag.

"That's where the queen keeps her crown," he snorts.

Evelyn's heart thuds. Her face prickles.

"Ignore him," she whispers to Queen. "He's mean."

"Or scared," Queen says.

Evelyn considers this. What would Connor be scared of? A name? A name is just a piece of air. It isn't real. Not the way a poisonous snake is real, or a car coming at you full speed.

"Scared of what?" she asks Queen.

Queen shrugs. "Of something he's afraid of."

Evelyn wrinkles her brow. Of course a person

is scared of the thing he's afraid of. That just goes round and round …

"That's a dog chasing its tail," she says. Then she feels foolish. Her mother has warned her to *keep a tight rein* on her imagination.

Queen won't know what she's talking about.

Queen looks at her and smiles.

"As long as it isn't chasing *my* tail," he says. His teeth are very white and very wide. They remind Evelyn of a washer and dryer.

Woof! Woof-woof!

The grade-five students flock to the classroom window.

There's a dog. A real one, frizzled and gray, sitting on a freshly painted hopscotch, thumping its tail.

Without asking Mr. Zhang for permission, Queen opens the window, puts two fingers in his mouth and whistles.

He shouts, "Quiet, Patti Smith!" and turns to Mr. Zhang. "She must have followed my scent."

Parker elbows Connor, plugs his nose and makes a face as if something smells terrible.

"Have you got some string?" Queen asks Mr. Zhang. "I'll leash her to the flagpole and call my dad."

"That's no corgi," Parker says.

"She's like a ball of steel wool," Anneline Hopkins giggles. "With legs."

"She's a mutt," Parker says. "A mongrel."

"Actually, she's a Heinz 57," Queen says. "One of the more famous mixed breeds."

Mr. Zhang reaches for his teacher scissors and cuts a length of string for Queen.

As soon as he's out the door, Mr. Zhang addresses the class.

"I expect you to be very welcoming to … to … Queen," he says, again muffling the last letter. "Show him around at recess, introduce him to your friends, invite him to your house for a play date."

"Grade fives are too old for play dates," Khalid protests.

"Well, for a visit, then," Mr. Zhang says.

"We're too young for visits," Anneline complains.

A second sprig of hair springs up on Mr. Zhang's head.

"Well, then, what do grade fives do?"

"We hang out," Anneline says. "Or just hang."

"Some kids chill," Khalid says. "A few chillax. That's a blend of chill and relax."

"I see," says Mr. Zhang. He rattles the pages in his hand. "Now, who doesn't have a quiz yet?"

After Queen returns, the classroom soon grows silent. The only sound is the scratching of the students' pencils filling in sums. Then a truck growls into the school parking lot.

Violin music blares from its open windows.

"Mozart," Mr. Zhang diagnoses.

"My dad," Queen says, leaping up. "His hearing isn't so good. The rigors of the road took their toll."

Connor peers through the window. Eyes bulging, he waves Parker over.

"You gotta see this!"

Everyone watches as a tall man steps down from the dented pickup. He's wearing a yellow ski toque, faded jeans splattered with paint, a white shirt that Evelyn is pretty sure is an undershirt, shiny silver earrings and dozens of silver bracelets. His arms swarm with tattoos.

There is even a tattoo on his neck. Some kind of bird, Evelyn thinks.

The man doesn't look anything like the other Hillsberry dads.

"You rascal!" the man booms, approaching Patti Smith. He pulls a penknife from his back pocket and cuts the dog free. Patti Smith runs circles around the flagpole, then jumps into the truck, barking twice — *Goodbye!* — in the direction of the classroom window.

Queen's dad revs the engine and chugs away, taking the sound of flutes and violins with him.

Tick. The minute hand spasms. The kids pick up their pencils again. Evelyn blinks at her quiz.

Numbers always act as they should, she thinks.

She kicks off her tight shoes. Her feet un-squish. Relief bubbles up in the spaces between her toes.

3

At recess, Evelyn joins her friends in the alcove by the double doors. They've been waiting since kindergarten to occupy this special spot, which by some unspoken rule is for grade fives only. The alcove is sheltered and private, and it has a good wall for handball. The planters make good benches, too, but you have to be careful about squashing the plants.

"I followed him when he went to the bathroom," Anneline is saying. "He used the Boys."

"My grandma's dog is named Queen," Isabella

volunteers. "She's a toy poodle. Her collar has real diamonds."

Connor balances along a planter, head high.

"Make way," he warbles in a stuffy English accent. He waves weakly. "Make way for the queen."

Everyone laughs except Evelyn. She glances at Queen, who is shooting baskets near enough to hear.

Does he hear them? She can't tell. He squats, puts his tongue between his washer-and-dryer teeth and pushes the ball away from his chest.

Every time, the ball bounces off the rim.

Evelyn walks over to him. Last year she played noon-hour basketball and got quite good.

"Use the backboard," she tells him. "It's called a bank shot."

Evelyn's mother often introduces her as *a shy lass* because she speaks so quietly. Over the summer, her friend Anneline kept telling her to speak up. At summer camp, when Evelyn asked Anneline to be her archery partner, she sighed, "I can't hear you, Evelyn," and skipped off with a girl named Kimmi.

But Queen has no trouble hearing her. He nods and adjusts his shot.

Bop-whoosh.

"Yay!" Queen jumps up and down. He and Evelyn high five each other. It's a perfect smack.

Evelyn's hand tingles as if it's electrified.

❧

Evelyn pretends she's walking home from the first day of school one hundred years ago. The problem is, the photos from a hundred years ago are all in black and white. But that was the camera's fault. The world wasn't black and white. The grass was green and the brick houses were red, just like now.

Squinting a little, she cancels out the cars and the telephone poles. The trees and birds stay. A man passes by on a bicycle. She replaces his helmet with a bowler hat.

"Wait up!" Queen rolls toward her on his skateboard. "Can I walk with you?"

Evelyn shakes her head. The telephone poles replant themselves. Queen's face falls.

"I was just clearing my mind," Evelyn says.

Queen tucks his skateboard under his arm. Evelyn looks around in case Anneline is watching.

"Do you like Hillsberry School?" she asks.

"I don't know yet. Mr. Zhang is nice. And some of the kids seem nice."

"Not all of them," she says, thinking of Parker and Connor.

"Some of them," Queen says, smiling.

As they pass under a tree, something clicks in the upper branches. A chestnut bounces down toward them. Queen reaches out to catch it but misses. He bends and picks it up from the ground.

Evelyn loves the feel of a chestnut in her hand. Like a springy stone. She looks for one, too.

"That might have been the first chestnut to fall this year," she says. She looks under the next tree. No luck. "Maybe the first in all of Hillsberry!"

"I wish I'd caught it. It could have been good luck."

"Or *bad* luck," Evelyn says. "Maybe if you caught it you would have triggered some spell. All of Hillsberry would have been turned into … into …"

"Saliva."

"Saliva?"

The two burst into laughter. Queen's laugh is like hard rain. Evelyn's is like a waterfall going backwards.

"Saliva from vampire bats might stop people's blood from clotting in their brains," Evelyn says. "It's called a stroke. My grandfather had one."

"People rub it on their heads or what?"

"I don't know. I just wonder how they get it from the bat."

"Maybe they wave yummy things under its nose. What would make a vampire drool? Blood sausage?"

"Stornoway black pudding." Evelyn shudders. "My mother makes it. Pig's blood and oatmeal."

"Where does she get the pig's blood?"

"She buys it at the butcher."

"My grandfather has a part of a pig in his heart. A valve from the pig's heart. They had to stop my grandpa's heart to do the operation. A machine took over."

"I hope he's okay," Evelyn says.

"Me, too. He snorts every so often. As a joke. *Oink oink*. It's called xenotransplantation."

"When an old man grunts like a pig?"

Queen laughs.

"Xenotransplantation is a transplant between species. Xeno means *stranger*," he explains.

"Like xenophobia."

"Yeah. Fear of strangers."

Evelyn thinks about xenophobia. Is that what Parker and Connor have? Is that why they teased Queen all day? They called his gym shorts disco shorts because they were shiny. But their basketball shorts were ridiculous. Way down past their knees. And shiny, too. A different kind of shiny, but still.

34

"I know about Xeno's Paradox," Evelyn says.

She read about it in one of the World Wonders books her grandparents sent her for her ninth birthday. *These were your mother's when she was a girl,* Grandma's card explained. As far as Evelyn can tell, her mother never read the books. The spines are stiff and her mom doesn't talk about any of the amazing stuff in the pages.

"A paradox is a puzzle."

"Yeah. This one says you can never get from one place to another."

"How does that work?"

"Well, for me to go home from school, I have to go halfway there, right?"

"Of course."

"Okay. So, halfway to my house from the school is the fire hall. To get to the fire hall, I have to go halfway there, too, right? Let's say this chestnut tree is the halfway point. And to get to this chestnut tree, I have to go halfway. Say, to the school fence. To get to the school fence, I also have to go halfway."

"To the swings."

"And halfway to the swings — "

"The bike rack."

"And halfway to the bike rack — "

"A gum splat."

"And halfway to that — "

"It goes on and on."

"For infinity. But it's just an idea," Evelyn says. "A math trick. I don't know what it has to do with strangers. Anyway, it isn't really true. I mean, we got here."

They're at the fire hall. A firefighter is polishing a fire truck's hubcap. He looks into it and whistles. "Aren't I handsome!"

Queen and Evelyn laugh.

"I go this way," Queen says, pointing with his chin.

"That way," Evelyn says, pointing *her* chin.

Queen jumps on his skateboard and zooms off. And Evelyn runs all the way home. That way she can get out of her tight shoes sooner.

4

Two weeks later, the ground is carpeted with chestnuts and the sky is like the underside of a frying pan. Gray and heavy. Evelyn has done up every button of her cardigan and wishes the sleeves were longer. If she breathes out from deep in her throat, she can see her breath.

Evelyn and Queen never meet on the way to school. Evelyn is already at her desk when he hurries through the classroom door, his long hair knotty from sleeping.

"We are spending the week in ancient Egypt,"

Mr. Zhang announces. "We'll write poems, put on plays, draw comics, even dance — "

"You're in a good mood, Mr. Zhang," Anneline says.

"You're right, Anneline. I am." Mr. Zhang's mouth wobbles.

"Did you get a puppy or something?"

Mr. Zhang's mouth bubbles into a smile. "No, not a puppy. I'm getting married."

"To who?" everyone asks.

"To *whom*," Mr. Zhang says. "To a very nice person. And that's all I'm going to say."

"Is she going to wear a poufy white dress?"

Mr. Zhang laughs. "No. Definitely not. And I'm not going to, either. Now, what do you know about ancient Egypt?"

"Mummies," Khalid calls out.

"Pyramids."

"Pharaohs!"

"Scarabs."

"The Sphinx."

"Hieroglyphics."

"I know what Queen likes about Egypt," Parker volunteers. "Cleopatra."

"And Nefertiti," Connor adds.

The two boys chuckle. Evelyn can't stand it. She raises her hand. She wants to change the subject.

Mr. Zhang looks pleased. She hardly ever talks in class.

"Teeth," she says, remembering a chapter of World Wonders.

"Teeth?" Connor smirks.

"The ancient Egyptians looked after their teeth. They had recipes for mouthwash, with frankincense and cumin. And some mummies have been found wearing braces. Gold wires holding their teeth together. Also, their teeth got ground down by all the desert sand that blew into their bread dough."

"Disgusting," Anneline says.

"Ancient Egyptian dentistry," Mr. Zhang says, writing in his notebook. "That's a new one."

~

The afternoon sky is white and wooly like a donkey's belly. Evelyn imagines a great donkey straddling the world. She's waiting for Queen so they can walk home together — as far as the fire hall, anyway.

Connor and Parker are by the school doors, peering into a cell phone. Queen comes out of the school. He walks differently from other kids. He rocks with each step, dips and rises, as if his knees are springs.

"Hey!" Parker calls. He raises the phone and yells, "Smile!"

Connor jumps on his bike and starts pedaling around Queen in tight circles. Parker and Connor have the nicest bikes in school, with sleek seats and heavy locks.

"You're in my way," Queen finally says.

Connor stops pedaling.

"Loser!" Parker calls after Queen. He holds his phone up. "Smile for the camera!"

Queen catches up with Evelyn.

"How was field hockey?" he asks her.

Evelyn's heart is pounding. But she pretends to be as calm as Queen is.

"Good," she says. She tries to smile. "How was chess/environment club?"

"Three people showed up! That's pretty good."

Queen started a club that meets one week to play chess and the next week to come up with a recycling plan for the school. Evelyn doesn't like chess, but the recycling ideas interest her. Queen says you have to join both.

The fire truck is heading out on a call. The firefighters wave as they pass by.

"Would you like to be a firefighter?" Queen asks Evelyn.

Evelyn laughs.

Anneline once asked her if she'd like to be a pop star. Her mom says she could work for the government one day. A desk job, like hers.

Maybe she'd like to be a dentist.

But a firefighter?

Evelyn imagines clomping through a burning house in rubber boots, helmet on her head, mask over her face, heavy water hose under her arm. She lumbers up a charred staircase. Her feet break twice through the charcoal steps. Her breathing sounds like Darth Vader's. A Dalmation dog starts to bark. It's in a small smoky room on its hind legs. Its front legs rest on a baby's crib. Evelyn takes the sleeping baby in her arms and hurries down the stairs — skipping the broken ones — and out onto the lawn. The baby wakes and howls, taking in great gulps of fresh air.

"A firefighter would be okay," Evelyn says. "What about you?"

"Nah. I'm going to be a nurse."

"A nurse is good. But what about a doctor? Or a surgeon? All those shiny instruments."

"Maybe. Dad cut his finger with the bread knife last year and the blood didn't bother me. And I liked dissecting a cow's eye at science camp."

"Do you like sewing?"

"Yeah." Queen smiles. "Yeah. I could be a surgeon. That could be awesome. Oh ..." He pulls a wrinkled envelope from his hoodie pocket. "My birthday party. Tomorrow. Sorry for the late notice. We do things last minute in my family. I hope you can come."

❧

At home, Evelyn hangs her cardigan in the hall closet and lines up her shoes by the door. A hole is wearing through the end of her right runner already. She hopes her mom won't see. If she does, she might put Evelyn back in loafers.

Every day, her mother leaves a glass of milk in the fridge and a plate of oatcakes on the counter. Evelyn peels the plastic wrap off them and sits at the kitchen table. The cold milk is sharp against her throat. It nearly hurts.

She has challenged herself not to open Queen's envelope until she's in her room. She can't rush. She chews at a normal speed and swings her feet back and forth the way she usually does. As if she has all the time in the world. She places her dishes in the sink and neatly folds up the squares

43

of plastic wrap for her mother to use again to-morrow. Then she heads upstairs, normal speed.

But halfway up the stairs, she starts to run, yanking her backpack buckles on the way.

The invitation is a funny picture made with magazine pictures. At the bottom it says *Collage by Queen*. Queen has stuck Abe Lincoln's long face onto a horse's body that's balanced on a duck's two legs. The creature stands on top of a refrigerator.

It's my birthday, Queen has written on the white fridge door.

Instead of a gift, bring two dollars
One dollar is for a ukulele, the other dollar
will help animals at the SPCA
From: After school
Until: 7 p.m.

A corner of Lincoln's hat is peeling. Evelyn gets her glue stick and presses it down. She pins the invitation to her bulletin board.

Queen must have made an original collage for each guest, she thinks. That's a lot of work.

5

Evelyn is sewing the tear on the toe of her right shoe when her mother comes home from work. Evelyn hurries downstairs and kisses her cheek as she always does.

It's hard, but she manages to wait for her mother to hang up her blazer and transfer her orthotics into her slippers.

"I'm invited to a birthday party," she blurts when her mother is ready.

"Whose birthday?"

"The new boy."

"What new boy?"

"Queen."

"Quinn, you mean."

"No, Queen."

"Quentin."

"Queen."

"That's not a boy's name."

"He's nice," Evelyn says. "Creative."

"I should guess he's creative with a name like that! Why on earth would his parents name him Queen? I mean, I could almost understand King. Or Prince. Isn't there a musician named Prince? A rock star?"

Evelyn itches with impatience. "Can I go?"

"Go where?"

"To the party."

"Right," her mother says. "Well."

She pauses. Evelyn feels like she's going to burst.

Finally, her mother nods. "When is it, then?"

"After school."

"Yes, but which day?"

"Tomorrow," Evelyn says, barely opening her mouth.

"Tomorrow? He doesn't give you much warning, this boy named Queen. How will we get a present in time?"

Evelyn explains about the two dollars, but her mother doesn't like it.

"I can't send you to a birthday party without a gift."

"But he said no gifts," Evelyn begs.

"Just a wee one. After supper we'll go to the mall." Evelyn's mom wanders into the kitchen. "I'll wash you an outfit tonight. Tomorrow already! A boy named Queen."

At least Evelyn's mother and father have something to talk about at supper. Usually the only sounds are of their cutlery across their plates. A knife sawing a pork chop, a fork chasing a pea.

ᜎ

Evelyn feels like she's wearing a costume. She feels like she's pretending to be someone she's not. But her mother wants her to wear a dress to Queen's party. And she didn't want to argue and maybe lose the chance to go. Her mother said the dress makes her look graceful. But it's the opposite. She feels clunky and stiff. The only thing keeping her from joining the weekend field hockey team is the uniform. That awful short skirt. Luckily, Girl Guides lets her choose between pants and a skirt. She chooses the pants.

But she's not allowed to go to Queen's birthday party in pants.

They went to the mall last night and bought Queen a small basketball hoop to clip over his bedroom door. It comes with a felt ball.

The present is now in a plastic bag in Evelyn's cubby. It is wrapped in brown paper that Evelyn covered with stickers of dogs.

Evelyn worked hard on the card. It's a drawing of Queen shooting baskets. She taped eight quarters between Queen's hands and the basket. They're supposed to be a ball traveling a perfect shot. The problem is that together the quarters are heavy. The card droops badly. Evelyn wishes she had chosen cardboard.

"You look nice," Anneline whispers from her desk. Then her eyes stick on Evelyn's near-runners.

Evelyn guesses the shoes don't match her green dress. Or maybe Anneline is staring at the knob of thread on the right toe. While mending, Evelyn got the idea to make room for her toe rather than simply shut the hole, so she created a kind of bubble, like a sideways hammock.

Who else is invited to Queen's party? Evelyn looks around the classroom. She doubts Parker or Connor were invited. They have started breaking Queen's pencils. They press the nibs against his desk until the pencil leads snap. They shoot across the desk and end up on the floor. Sometimes kids step on the nibs and leave black streaks on the floor tiles.

Parker and Connor even took Queen's lunch once. Right out of his backpack.

"You should tell Mr. Zhang," Evelyn told him.

"It's okay. I tell my parents all about it," he said. Then he laughed. "Parker and Connor are going to be surprised by what's in the Tupperware. Brussels sprouts and a quinoa burrito."

Evelyn doesn't like Brussels sprouts. They taste like her fingers taste after she's held her house key for a while.

When the buzzer sounds at the end of the day, Queen and Evelyn set off together straight from the classroom. Usually they meet at the corner.

In the schoolyard, Parker and Connor are at the bicycle rack that looks to Evelyn like a giant half-submerged potato masher.

Parker sees them first.

"Here comes the queen!" he sings, lifting an imaginary trumpet into the air and squawking a royal fanfare.

"And," Connor pronounces, looking at Evelyn, "*her* lady in waiting."

Evelyn flushes with heat. She's embarrassed. She trembles. She's angry. But she's not mad at Connor and Parker. She's mad at Queen! This is *his* fault. If he didn't have such a strange name. If he wore clothes like everyone else, and didn't start clubs.

Kids don't start clubs. Teachers start clubs.

As they pass the boys, Connor pushes Queen's skateboard from under his arm. It goes rolling across the schoolyard.

Evelyn is afraid Connor is going to hit Queen. Maybe he's going to hit *her*!

Queen walks calmly toward his skateboard and picks it up. He's ... graceful, Evelyn thinks. Connor and Parker are taller than Queen but Queen seems bigger than them.

Queen looks back at Evelyn.

"Ignore them," he says.

Wasn't that what Evelyn told *him* on the first day of school?

She's too upset to answer. She vows not to cry, but tears sting her eyes and her nose tingles. She wants to curl up right there on the sidewalk.

Queen glances at her every few steps.

"It'll be okay," he says.

"No, it won't!"

All day, Evelyn has been looking forward to going to Queen's house. Now she just wants to go home. And find a glass of cold milk waiting

51

for her in the fridge and a plate of oatcakes on the counter.

Queen stops. "You don't have to come if you don't want to."

Queen's eyes are so green, Evelyn thinks. Like summer ponds. She looks for her favorite freckles — the angular, umber one on the bridge of his nose and the milk chocolate smattering on his chin.

Queen smiles. His smile makes Evelyn laugh.

The thing is, she thinks, Queen is the nicest boy in the world. And today is his birthday!

"How do you stand it?" she asks once they're walking again.

"I put up a force field. All around me. The dumb things they say — even the dumb things they *think* — bounce off it."

"I'd like a force field like that."

"Just make one. Imagine it. *See* it. Mine is turquoise."

Evelyn closes her eyes. She imagines electricity spreading out from her, pushing Parker and Connor and their stupid words out, out, out.

It's like she's in an egg with a strong shell. It's blue.

She opens her eyes again. She feels great!

"The force field works for good things, too," Queen says. "But the opposite way. If someone says something nice to you, the field lets it in. Right into your heart."

6

The walk to Queen's house is longer than Evelyn expected. They climb over fences and cross grassy fields. They even go through a small forest.

Finally, they arrive at a wide gravel road without sidewalks. It's a long way between houses.

Evelyn's left foot aches. She thinks she might stitch a sideways hammock on that shoe, too.

Queen's house is big but not fancy. Three brown chickens bob about in the front yard. They rush over to peck at Evelyn's shoes.

Queen laughs. "They think the laces are worms."

Patti Smith pounces when they step through the front door, wagging her tail so fast Evelyn thinks she can hear it whir against the air, like the rope when she skips pepper.

"Down!" Queen tells Patti Smith.

Evelyn stares around her. The walls are painted red and filled with paintings. The air is warm and smells like flowers and cinnamon. A real fire crackles in the fireplace, and the bookshelves overflow. Gentle music pours from speakers that hang from the ceiling.

Evelyn spies a purple velvet couch with little mirrors stitched into it. You'd never see anything like it at Moods, where her father sells furniture.

Queen drapes his hoodie on the head of a giraffe sculpture, and Evelyn does the same with her cardigan. They hang their backpacks from the giraffe's neck. Evelyn adds her shoes to the pile by the door.

"I like the embroidery on the toe of your shoe," Queen says.

"I was mending a hole."

"It's the shape of Iceland."

"They're too small. My toe is pushing through."

"What size are your feet?"

"Five. But these are four and a half."

"I used to be a five. I'm a six now."

"Son!" A woman with hair even shorter than Evelyn's bursts into the hall and gathers Queen into her arms. "Birthday boy!" She breathes in. "You smell good. Like sunshine."

The woman thrusts her hand toward Evelyn. "I'm Marianne, Queen's mom."

Evelyn shakes Marianne's hand, trying hard not to stare at the flowers and vines that wind from her wrist to her shoulder.

Evelyn realizes she has never touched someone with tattoos. She's never touched a tattoo! Now she has.

"I've heard a lot about you, Evelyn," Marianne says.

Evelyn catches her reflection in a mirror and stares. What is there to tell?

Marianne ruffles Queen's hair. "Come find me in the studio in half an hour. I have a project for you."

Queen's dad is in the kitchen, wearing an apron, pots steaming all around him. He sets his slurpy whisk on the counter and lifts Queen high until his head hits the ceiling.

Bonk.

"Birthday bump," his dad says. He hoists Queen nine more times.

Bonk, bonk, bonk, bonk, bonk, bonk, bonk, bonk, bonk.

"Ow," says Queen. "Ow, ow, ow, ow, ow, ow, ow, ow, ow."

"I'm Rodney," Queen's dad tells Evelyn, putting out his hand.

His tattoos are designs rather than pictures. Swirls and knots and mazes. She was right about the bird on his neck. Up close, she can see that it's black with a ruffle of feathers around its shoulders.

"Raven," she says. She clamps her hand over her mouth.

"Well done. Most people think it's a crow." He picks up his whisk. "One woman even asked if it was a pigeon!"

He and Evelyn laugh.

"I'm making your favorites, Queen. Potato latkes and bangers. Perfect for a tenth birthday."

Evelyn can't believe it. Her father never cooks. He barbecues thin steaks once in a while in the summer, but that's it.

Rodney sends her and Queen to the henhouse to gather eggs. Evelyn doesn't like reaching under the chickens. She doesn't like to bother them, but she loves the warm weight of the eggs that sit perfectly in the palms of her hands.

Back in the kitchen, she and Queen grate ten potatoes. Evelyn wonders who else is coming to the party.

"You're the only person I invited," Queen says, as if he can read her mind. "We moved around a lot before we came here. I even spent some of my birthdays in hotel rooms! Usually I'd just celebrate my birthday with my parents. I've never had a big party."

When they've grated a damp, shaggy tower of potato, they cross the large backyard to a shed, which Marianne has turned into a pottery studio.

"She always wanted to be a potter, but life on the road made it impossible. You can't have a kiln in a hotel room."

Inside, a cat snoozes on an armchair with scuffed legs and stuffing fizzing out of the holes in the upholstery. Evelyn can't stop staring at the chair. She has never seen such a used-up old thing in someone's house.

Marianne looks up from her wheel. A drop of clay clings to her cheek.

"There you are," she says. She puts a lump of clay in Evelyn's hands, which are still sticky with potato juice. The clay is a strange yellow.

"It's local." Marianne points out the dirty window to a pit in the yard with a shovel beside it. "Hyper local. Super easy to work with and it doesn't crack easily when it's fired."

Marianne shows Evelyn how to use the potter's wheel. Evelyn can't believe how smooth and soft the clay becomes, spinning under her hands. How easy it is to shape. Like it's alive!

"It'll be easy for you to pick something for Share and Hype," Evelyn says to Queen as they etch designs into their soup bowls with tooth-picks. "Everything here is so … cool."

At school, Mr. Zhang announced they would be doing Show and Tell next week. Anneline said they were too old for Show and Tell, so Mr. Zhang suggested they give it a different name. The class came up with Share and Hype.

"You must have *something* cool in your house," Queen says.

"An old cream jug. That's it. It was my mother's great-aunt's second husband's grand-mother's. It's over a hundred and fifty years old. Silver. We never use it."

"Is it nice?"

"Mom keeps it shiny. But it's still just a cream jug."

"You could fill it with cream. Pour out little cups for everyone. Put it to work."

Evelyn likes the idea. She can show what the jug *does*, not just what it looks like. She smiles to herself.

If her mom saw her, she would say, "Well, don't you look like the cat that got the cream?"

7

Even though Evelyn is the only guest, there are lots of presents for Queen.

"Let's eat first," Marianne says.

The room is flooded with candlelight. It makes the air thick and dreamy. Evelyn counts the candles as Marianne lights them. Eighteen in all, each one in a different candleholder.

Rodney puts on music that makes Evelyn think of snake charmers. Then he serves supper. On each plate is a single sausage beside a pancake, spelling out the number ten. The pancake is made out of grated potatoes.

There's an extra plate.

"For Patti Smith," Rodney says, winking at Evelyn as the dog hops up on the chair and gobbles down her meal. "Only on special occasions. And Sundays."

When her plate is clean, Patti Smith lies under the table, pressing warmly against Evelyn's feet.

Evelyn eyes the wrapped presents. She reads the labels. *From Uncle Gerry. From Aunt Daffodil.*

Then she gets a shock. One of the presents is addressed to "Queen Peter." Another is just for "Peter."

"Peter?" She stares at Queen. She can't believe it.

"It's my legal name."

"He's been Queen since he was four," Marianne says. "He had a robe then. Purple velour — "

"Velvet," Queen corrects.

"No, velour, I'm afraid."

"I thought it was velvet." Queen frowns.

"Well, it was still very soft and regal," his mom says. She turns to Evelyn. "It had gold embroidery on the hem. Queen wore it everywhere

— to the supermarket, to the library, even Tiny Tots soccer. He demanded to be called Queen. The name stuck."

"But the kids tease him!" Evelyn says.

Marianne frowns. "A lot?"

"No," Queen says.

"He just lets it bounce off," Evelyn says.

"My name is handy. I watch how people act when they hear it for the first time. It shows me what kind of people they are."

"So you test people," Evelyn says. "And they don't even know?"

"Not on purpose. It's just an extra. *You* never teased me, Evelyn, or even seemed to notice. I trusted you right away."

Evelyn blushes. She remembers what Queen said about letting the good things in. All the way in.

Queen opens his gifts: a book called *Rooftoppers*, a colorful patchwork hoodie, a Harry Potter Lego set, a harmonica, a baking soda rocket kit and the mini basketball hoop.

Rodney brings out the birthday cake and starts singing "Happy Birthday." His voice is so loud that Evelyn almost covers her ears. When she joins in it's like Rodney makes room for her voice, lets it wind around his.

Then Marianne joins in. Her voice is like a river, Evelyn thinks. Rodney's is like a stormy ocean.

Queen blows out all the candles with one easy breath. The cake is blackberry cheesecake. Rodney says it has a little bit of rum in it, but not a lot. Evelyn won't mention that to her parents.

After they eat their cake, Queen and Evelyn decide to put up the basketball net.

As they head up the stairs, Marianne and Rodney do something Evelyn has never, ever seen her parents do. Rodney pushes back his chair and Marianne sits on his lap. They put their arms around each other and stay like that, talking and laughing. Even kissing! Evelyn stares until Queen calls her a second time to follow him up the stairs.

The net fits over Queen's door, and he and Evelyn take turns trying to sink the felt ball.

After a while, Marianne calls them down to the "Gibson Room." It's in the basement. The small room is filled with musical instruments. Marianne points out an electric guitar.

"The *pièce de résistance*," she says.

"The jewel in the crown," Rodney adds.

"The Big Kahuna," Queen says.

Evelyn thinks for a moment. "The prize haggis."

Everyone laughs.

It's a 1964 Gibson, Rodney explains, which doesn't mean anything to Evelyn, but she knows to say "Wow."

Marianne points Evelyn toward the drum set and sits at the piano. Evelyn taps lightly at the cymbals and pushes delicately on a foot pedal. She presses harder. *Bang!* Harder. *Woo!*

Queen looks around for an instrument.

"Under the couch," Marianne directs. Queen gets down on his knees and pulls out a bundle wrapped in a beach towel.

"It's the ukulele, isn't it? It's the ukulele!"

"Yup," Marianne says.

Queen strums his new instrument, Rodney twangs a few long notes on the Gibson, and Marianne leans into the microphone and starts to sing a song about fishing.

You get a line and I'll get a pole, honey,
You get a line and I'll get a pole, babe ...

Evelyn taps the little drum, the big drum, then the cymbal.

Tap-bang-smash.

And again. *Tap-bang-smash.*

Tap-bang-smash. Tap-bang-smash. Tap-bang-smash. Tap-bang-SMASH.

❧

It's time to go home. Rodney and Marianne are cleaning the kitchen. Evelyn is looking for her second shoe, the one with the hammock toe.

She hears a sigh and a rustle in the next room and peeks in.

Patti Smith is holding Evelyn's shoe between her front paws and licking it.

Evelyn laughs. She tugs the shoe out from Patti Smith's paws.

The room she's in is an office, with a desk and computer and filing cabinet. Framed on the wall are gold and silver disks, like flat Frisbees.

Evelyn takes a closer look.

A plaque under one of the circles says, *Gold Record. Presented to The Sky Warriors for the album ROAD TO EVERYWHERE. Half a million copies sold.*

Another says, *Platinum Record. Presented to The Sky Warriors for the album TUMBLE-DOWN. Over one million copies sold.*

Evelyn sucks in. She knows The Sky Warriors. Her father turns up their music when they come on the radio.

A photo on the wall shows five men with long hair and beards. Evelyn recognizes the man holding the guitar. He looks younger, but it's definitely him. There's the raven tattoo. And the 1964 Gibson.

"Your mother's here!" Queen calls.

Evelyn hurries to the front door. She gets her sweater on quickly while her mother and Marianne talk about the rain. Evelyn can tell her mother is trying not to look at Marianne's tattoos. She hopes Rodney doesn't come out to say hello. One at a time.

"The sky's about to break," Evelyn's mother says. "It will be a downpour."

"Cats and dogs," Marianne says.

"And chair legs," adds Evelyn's mom.

Evelyn tugs her mother out the door.

"Hold on! We forgot the goody bag!" Queen yells as they get into the car.

He runs back into the house.

Evelyn hears him call, "Paper bag! A big one!"

Moments later, he hands a bulky package through the car window.

"Thanks for coming," he says. "See you at school."

"Happy birthday," Evelyn says. She hugs the goody bag to her chest.

Evelyn's mom glances at her. "Did you have a good time?"

"Yes."

"Who else was at the party?"

"No one."

"No one?"

"Just me."

"Just you?"

"Yep."

"I see."

But Evelyn doesn't think her mother does see. Not quite. Her mother thinks it's sad that Queen had only one guest.

Evelyn looks out the car window, nodding in time with the telephone wire swooping up, down, up, down between the poles.

"It wasn't sad," she says. "It was wonderful."

8

Evelyn manages to wait until she's in her pajamas, face washed and teeth brushed, even tomorrow's outfit laid out on the end of her bed, before she tears open the gigantic goody bag.

Inside are two potato pancakes wrapped in waxed paper, the drum sticks she used in the Gibson Room, a Polaroid photo that Marianne took of her at the drums. And, at the bottom of the bag, the *pièce de résistance*. A pair of runners! Red, with blue stars on the sides, and nearly new. Size five.

They fit perfectly. Evelyn races across her room and, twisting in mid-air like a high jumper, lands — *whumpf!* — on her back on her bed.

Tomorrow's outfit bounces up and scatters on the floor.

"What are you doing up there?" her dad yells from the living room.

"Nothing," Evelyn answers, out of breath. "Just having some fun!"

Before she turns off her light, Evelyn studies the photo for a long time.

She looks different. She stares, trying to figure out why.

It's her freckles. They are no longer the colors of weak tea and hay.

Somehow, her freckles have turned copper and gold.

ᔕ

Evelyn is allowed to take her mother's great-aunt's second husband's grandmother's sterling silver cream jug for Share and Hype. It's bundled up in three layers of bubble wrap.

With her own money, Evelyn buys Dixie cups and a large carton of cream at the convenience store down the street.

On Monday she puts everything carefully into her backpack. Her mother drives her to school. Evelyn does all she can to make sure her mother doesn't see the red runners on her feet.

"The clouds look like smoke today," she says as they walk to the car.

Her mother stops and looks up. "You get white smoke like that when you burn coal."

"What do you have to burn to get cotton candy?" Evelyn asks.

Her mother laughs. "Cherry blossoms?"

As they drive along, Evelyn thinks about the cream in her backpack, sloshing around in its carton. As they drive past the convenience store, she gets a brainwave.

"Mom! Can I get something at the store?"

"What?"

"It's a secret. But I'll tell you later. I promise."

"A secret and a promise. All in one gulp."

Evelyn bites her lip.

Her mother reaches into her purse. "Will five dollars be enough?"

Evelyn runs into the store. When she gets back to the car, her mother is frowning. She tips her chin toward Evelyn's feet.

"Where are those from?"

"From … from Queen."

"What about your new shoes?" her mother asks.

"They're a bit small."

Evelyn buckles up. Her mother says nothing as she starts the engine.

"I like these shoes," Evelyn says finally. "They're comfortable. They have bounce."

Her mother pulls the car up to the school. Girls pass by, some wearing scuffed ballet shoes, others in runners. Then Isabella crosses in front of them in her pink jeans and a feathery jacket. On her feet she wears boots with heels. The heels are so high they click against the pavement.

Evelyn raises her eyebrows and looks at her mother. Her mother raises her eyebrows and looks at Evelyn.

"I won't ever wear those," Evelyn says.

Her mother laughs. She leans over and kisses Evelyn on the cheek.

∾

Khalid is first up for Share and Hype. He shows off a Lego City set called Deep Sea Helicopter.

Anneline hypes a first-place dance ribbon.

Parker presents a basketball signed by the famous basketball player Steve Nash. Mr. Zhang is impressed.

"Where did you meet Steve Nash?" he asks.

"I didn't," Parker answers. "My dad bought the ball on eBay."

As he puts the ball back into his cubby, Evelyn notices something that makes her heart jump.

It's a sticker on his lunchbox. A picture of five men on a highway. The Sky Warriors.

It's her turn to Share and Hype. Queen is in the front row and says a loud "Wow!" when she unwraps the cream jug. A few kids get hold of the bubble wrap, but Mr. Zhang can't figure out who is playing with it.

"This jug was made in 1885," Evelyn starts. *Pop. Pop.* "The same year the Canadian Pacific Railway was finished — "

"The last spike," Mr. Zhang murmurs.

"The same year the Statue of Liberty arrived in New York."

Pop. Pop.

"*And* Jumbo the P. T. Barnum Circus elephant was killed in a train wreck."

"Aww," the students croon.

"And Sarah E. Goode invented the first hide-away bed. The bed folded up into a desk!"

Pop. Pop.

"It's sterling silver — "

Khalid raises his hand. "How many troy ounces?"

"One point eight." Good thing she looked it

up on antiques.com. She points out the initials SS stamped into the side of the jug.

"It was made in England by Stanley Smith silversmiths."

Pop. Pop.

"Who would like a taste of cream?"

The popping stops.

The students push and bump the desks as they line up for their Dixie cups.

But when Evelyn tips the jug for the first time, they go so quiet you could hear a new pin drop.

They can't believe their eyes.

The cream is purple! Food coloring was Evelyn's secret.

Sure, a few kids wrinkle their noses and say *yuck*.

But Evelyn doesn't let a few *yucks* bother her. She just lets in the *oohs*.

SARA CASSIDY is a journalist and editor and the author of fourteen books for young readers, including *A Boy Named Queen*. Her recent work includes the picture book *Helen's Birds*, illustrated by Sophie Casson. Sara's books have been selected for the Junior Library Guild, and she has been a finalist for the Chocolate Lily Award, the Bolen Books Children's Book Prize, the Rocky Mountain Book Award, the Diamond Willow Award, the Ruth and Sylvia Schwartz Children's Book Award, the Manitoba Young Readers' Choice Award and the Silver Birch Express Award. She has also won a National Magazine Award (Gold) for a piece in *Today's Parent*. She lives in Victoria.

www.saracassidywriter.com